Quarto is the authority on a wide range of topics.

Quarto educates, entertains and enriches the lives of
our readers—enthusiasts and lovers of hands-on living.

www.quartoknows.com

First published in the United States of America in 2016 by
Race Point Publishing, a member of
Quarto Publishing Group USA Inc.
142 West 36th Street, 4th Floor
New York, New York 10018
quartoknows.com

10 9 8 7 6 5 4 3 2 1

ISBN 978-1-63106-324-4

Editorial Director: Jeannine Dillon
Managing Editor: Erin Canning
Project Editor: Jason Chappell
Art Director: Merideth Harte
Design: Ashley Prine

Printed in China

PEOPLE

ELIZABETH "LIZZY" BENNET
The Smart, Sarcastic Heroine

JANE BENNET
The Hot Sister Who Doesn't
Know She's Hot

MARY BENNET
The Nerd Sister

CATHERINE "KITTY" BENNET
The Sister No One
Remembers Because She
Has No Point in the Plot

LYDIA BENNET
The Extremely Naughty Sister
(YOU KNOW!)

MRS. BENNET
The Money-Hungry Mom

MR. BENNET
The Disinterested Dad

MR. DARCY
The Handsome Hero

MR. BINGLEY
The Hero's Best Friend

PEOPLE

CAROLINE BINGLEY
The Mean Girl

LOUISA HURST
The Other Mean Girl
(she's marginally nicer)

CHARLOTTE LUCAS
The Spinster (she's 27)

WICKHAM
The Smooth Talker

GEORGIANA DARCY
The Hero's Shy Sister

LADY CATHERINE
DE BOURGH
The Hero's Rich and
Mean Aunt

ANNE DE BOURGH
The Ever-Sick Daughter of
Lady Catherine

MR. GARDINER
The Good Uncle

MRS. GARDINER
The Good Aunt

PEOPLE

COLONEL FITZWILLIAM
The Big Mouth

SOLDIERS
The Possibilities

COLONEL FORSTER
The Responsibility Taker

LADY LUCAS
The Gloater

SIR LUCAS
The Knighted One

MR. COLLINS
The Worst

PLACES

NETHERFIELD PARK

LONGBOURN

LUCAS LODGE

PEMBERLEY

MERYTON VILLAGE

ROSINGS

HUNSFORD

LONDON

BRIGHTON

"It is a truth universally acknowledged that a single man in possession of a good fortune must be in want of a wife."

Mr. Bingley, a single, handsome, and wealthy young man rents an estate called Netherfield Park in the county Hertfordshire. The local families, as a matter of custom, politeness, and occasionally self-serving interest, call on him. Among those families is the Bennets, with their five beautiful daughters. In Mr. Bingley's coterie are his sisters, his brother-in-law, and the pretentious Mr. Darcy, whom we will learn quite a bit about through the course of our tale.

Did you hear someone named Bingley rented ?

Yeah, so?

 SO!? So go introduce yourself!

Why?

WHY!!?!?! For your daughters! To be polite! BECAUSE IT'S WHAT YOU DO!

Ugh, those girls. SO ANNOYING. Lizzy is the only good one.

You're a real jerk sometimes.

– Tue, Oct 1, 10:12 AM –

 refuses to meet and now one of Mrs. Long's dumb nieces will snag him.

We'll get to meet him at the ball in like 2 weeks. Chill.

Ugh, he keeps bringing Bingley up just to taunt me. And Kitty WILL NOT STOP COUGHING!

You really need to relax. What does Mary think?

Don't you think  should go see Mr. Bingley?

 Well??? Isn't it the proper thing to do?

 NEVERMIND! I don't even care anymore.

– Wed, Oct 2, 3:44 PM –

  Hey.

Hi.

 Um, ?

– Wed, Oct 16, 10:12 AM –

  is pretty cute.

Totally. I can't believe you danced TWICE!!

 I know! But that Darcy. What a !!!

Right? I can't even.

 Well, who cares what he says, you're totally !!! And everyone thought he was a stuck-up snob cuz he IS!

Let's just never think about him again.

looked great the other night!

Thanks.

 I saw dance with her first.

Yup.

 Yes, a real looker.......

Your girls looked lovely, too.

DIDN'T THEY!?!?! THANK YOU!!!! !!! They are just so beautiful. And smart. And cultured. Oh, and how they dance! 🎩😊 danced with 👵 twice. TWICE!!! 💜 💜 💜 She really is such a beautiful young woman, any man would be lucky to have her. We'd love her to marry a man with such........means. 💲

I heard 🎩 say 👱 was the hottest girl at the ball. 💜 😍 👍

He danced with you, too, though

Well, he danced with lots of girls, but your sister. Wow! That 🧑 though. What a 💩!!

Everyone keeps saying that! But whatever. I don't even care. 🙄

– Fri, Oct 18, 5:07 PM –

Let's hang out with 👧 🙄 while we're here. They're the best we're going to get in this hick town. 😴 🙄

Yeah, fine. But their mother, 🤑 . UGH! She's the W.O.R.S.T!!!! 🔫 ⚰️ 👏

LOL! Right!? Could she be more vulgar? 💩 💩 💩 😈

👱‍♀️ is cool though. 👍 As long as she goes elsewhere to 💍 👰 😈 .

– Mon, Nov 4, 2:18 PM –

  better show a little leg or something if she wants to keep  interested!

!?!?

LOL!!! JK! She's just so dang cool .
She could be talking to my grandpa!
She needs to raise the 🌡 a little.
Let  know she likes him.

Sigh. I know. If I were her, I'd put a little sauce on it. But 😑 = 😑. That's just how she is.

Meanwhile,  keeps creeping up on my convos. 😠

Only  knows .

What a !! I'm going to let him have it before I lose my nerve. 😵

Cool. But then let's jam!!! 🎹 🎵 🖤 🖤

Ugh, really!? OK. Fine. 🙁

– Fri, Nov 8, 7:46 PM –

 I hanging out with you young folks. You should dance with ! Come on, it'd be fun.

Um, Ok . . .

– Fri, Nov 8, 7:47 PM –

 Elizabeth, you should dance with !

Hard pass.

This place sucks!

Actually, I wasn't thinking that at all. I was thinking about . She has such nice eyes. 😍

HER!?!?!

Her.

Whatever. Good luck with her mother when you marry her since you love her so much. 🐉 💩 🕷 👧

OMG! OMG! OMG! Did you see all the 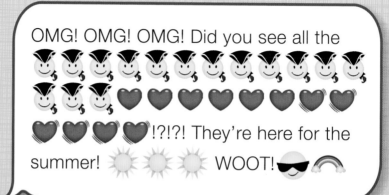!?!?! They're here for the summer! WOOT!

We have to go to  like RIGHT NOW!!!

Can I go to  for lunch with ?

YES!! Go now! Take the , and then when it 💧💧, you won't be able to get back. Sleepover!! 🌙💤 YESSSSS!

Jeez, can't I just take the ?? Please!?

No. = NOW!!!

Ugh, I'm so sick from that ride yesterday! 🤒 🥴

Oh no!! 😦 I'm on my way! �’ I'm going to walk 👻 and 👒 up near 🏚️, then I'll run right over.

Wed, Nov 13, 8:06 PM

Didn't 😓 look gross when she got here? FILTHY and SO sweaty!! 😬 😬 😬

I thought she looked fit. 💪

I'm going to stay at  to take care of Jane. 😠 💁 aren't so bad actually. They 🖤 👧 !

👋👍👍👍👍 YES!!! We are in! 💰

 Scratch that. They're terrible. 🙁

Just be cool! I'm coming tomorrow with and the doc. 💉

Hey! So, um, can we maybe have a party at your house? You totally said we could! 🙏💃🥂

Oh, right. Sure! 👍 But let's wait until 👵 is better. 👍? 😷

Oh, totally! She's going to be fine. Doc said so. Captain Carter, who is totally 🔥🔥🔥, will be back by then, 😍. So, ball at 🏛️???

You bet!

Hey, handsome! How goes it?

I'm fine.

 Wow! You typed that so fast! You sure are tapping something out!

No, not really. I just hate typing. I'm emailing my sister .

 Ok. Well, tell her I miss her!!!!

Why, so you can make fun of my moves? I don't think so.

K

Come walk with me.

Here in the living room? Er . . . OK.

Come walk with us.

Nope. Then you couldn't strut for me like you're doing, so what would be the point?

Send the , I am ready to get out of here!

Ummmm, no ...... The can't get there 'til Tuesday.

MOTHER! I KNOW that's not true! SEND IT!!!!!

Ugh, fine. I'll send it tomorrow. You know you're my least favorite child, right?

Glad you're feeling better but I'll miss you!

Me too! I can't wait for the ball.

Ugh. I'll only talk to you.

That can't be true. Oh, says to say .

I miss you already!!!

Hey, cuz! I hope you got that email I sent. I'll be getting to at 4 today!

Great.

I can't wait to tell you about my awesome new gag!!

I mean GIG. This freakin' phone is the work of the devil!!!!

Great.

And meet your lovely daughters.

Great.

– Mon, Nov 18, 8:09 AM –

 My cousin, , is coming to visit.

UGH!! THAT !! HATE!!!!!!

 It's not his fault that he'll inherit when I kick it.

It's not NOT his fault!!!!!

 What???

YOU HEARD ME!!!

– Mon, Nov 18, 4:22 PM –

 Your daughters are gorgeous!!!

Well, they won't be so cute when they're kicked out of their home, living on the street like filthy beggars!!!

Oh, well, now I wouldn't worry about that. Like I said, they're hot!

Oh! Right! They're totally hot!!

 Especially !

Try again.

 Especially !

– Tue, Nov 19, 4:47 PM –

You know when we were in today with 👀 🎀, before we went to Mrs. Philips's house?

Of course! That's when we saw !! 😍 How could I forget!? 💓

Did you see their faces when 🙂 and 🙂 noticed each other? I thought Darcy was going to pass out 😵 and Wickham was going to barf 🐵!

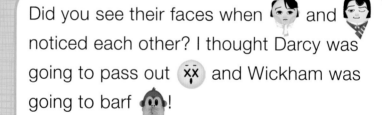

Really? That's super weird. . . . Do you think will ever shut up about his boss, ?

Do you think he'll ever shut up at all?

– Wed, Nov 20, 5:31 PM –

 Hey, girl!!

Oh, hi! How are you?

 OK......Seeing was kind of lame.

Ugh, everyone around here thinks he's a . How do you even know him??

I'm not really one to talk smack, but he's definitely a ! My dad and old Mr. Darcy were bros. Then me and old Mr. Darcy were , which totally pissed off I guess. I was supposed to get mad when his dad died.

But . . . ?

  was all about the . And whatever. It's weird. But I don't like to talk . Especially cuz his dad was so cool.

That's GROSS! should be stoned in the streets! Boooooooooo!

I can't believe what an utter jerk was to !!!

You sure there isn't some misunderstanding?

Doubt it! But W.E.! I'm going to dance with at the ball! also told me 's boss, , is 's aunt, and her daughter, , and are going to get married and make one giant estate. Take that, !

No wonder is always ! I can't wait to dance with !!!

You are going to the ball at ? I didn't think you church guys could dance.

Oh, heck yeah we do! How about you and me dance the first two?

Sure.

This ball is amazing!! I'm having the best time EVER!! 😍 🎉 💃

I guess. Have you seen ?

No . . . BTW, insists is mad cool no matter what anyone says.

Of course he said that!

 ?

Sure, why not? It's not like is here to dance with.

 That guy might not be as cool as you think.

Uh-huh.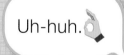

- Tue, Nov 26, 7:21 PM -

I hear you 🖤 !!! You should know, and I'm only saying this as a friend, that he is not that great. He's kind of the worst, actually. And a liar. 👖🔥😨

Because he was the son of a servant to old Mr. Darcy???? Is that it!?! Real classy. 👍🏿

WHATEVER! I was just trying to let you know he's a 😾. But FINE! You know best. ✌️

From: Mrs. Bennet

To: Lady Lucas

CC: All contacts

Subject: Here comes the bride!!!!

Hey, girl!

Jane is TOTALLY going to marry Mr. Bingley. SCORE!!

xoxoxox

Mrs. B

From: Elizabeth

To: Mrs. Bennet

Subject: RE: Here comes the bride!!!!

MOM!!!! YOU SENT THAT TO PRETTY MUCH EVERYONE!!! SO EMBARRASSING!!!

From: Mrs. Bennet

To: Elizabeth

Subject: RE: RE: Here comes the bride!!!!

LOL! Whoops! Oh well.

Great breakfast!!! Sooooo, I'd like to talk to 1on1. :)

 I'll get everyone out of here.

Ugh, keeps trying to follow me!! Girl can NOT take a hint.

 LOL! NP

SO, I have talked to your parents, and we have agreed that you should be my . Reasons being 1. As a member of the , I must have a wife. 2. I'd be super . 3. thinks I should get married and she is super smart . 4. Since I'm getting , I should definitely marry one of the Bennet girls. Phew! Glad that's settled !!!

Whoa, I didn't answer yet! Thanks, but no thanks.

Whatevs. I know you have to play hard to get. It's what the ladies do. No sweat! I can wait until you say yes.

No means no.

 Sure it does!

I'm being deadly serious. NO. NO. NO. NO. NO!

 You're so cute!!

- Wed, Nov 27, 10:17 AM -

 Congratulations!!!!!

She's playing hard to get, so it's not exactly a done deal. But I'm sure she'll come around. She's just being a woman. You know how women are!

 •••

Ugh,  can be such a PITA!! So stubborn! Don't worry though. I'll get her to come around.

If she's that much of a pain, I'm not sure I want to go through with this......

 Oh, no, that's not what I meant!!! She's awesome!!!! Super cool girl!!! Just leave this to me!

- Wed, Nov 27, 10:19 AM -

 Talk some sense into your daughter! She said NO to 's proposal. =

Good for her! That guy is .

Why are you THE WORST!?!?!?

- Wed, Nov 27, 10:21 AM -

 Marry or I'll never see you again !

For real!?!?!

 Well, pick me or your mom, cause if you marry , I'll never see you again .

LOL! I'm going with you on this one, Dad.

Yeah, so about the whole  thing. JK!

 It's cool. Maybe the whole thing was my bad. If so, sorry! If not, no worries! 😀

- Wed, Nov 27, 12:17 PM -

I can't believe your obstinate sister  is RUINING this family!!!! What's wrong with Mr. Collins anyway!?!?!? I think he's perfectly nice.

Why do I even try talking to you? I give up!!!!!

Ugh, close call with . That man =

Oh, I dunno, he's not SO bad.

 Well, we're all super grateful you actually can stand to talk to the man!! THANK YOU!! 🙏

NP!

Hey, sorry we didn't get to at the ball. I just couldn't stand to be in the same room as stupid 😭!! 💩 😡

OMG, I totally understand! Why don't you come to 🏛 with me and 👵. You can meet 💰 and 👴. It'll be . . . cool? LOL!

Awesome! 👍

- Thu, Nov 28, 4:15 PM -

Hey! So we took off for 🏛️. Sorry we didn't get to say goodbye!!! We are just DYING to see 👧's sister, 👶.

Oh. OK . . . Have fun. I'll miss you!!!

👶 is SUPER cool 😎 and 🎩👶 really wants to hang out with her. 😍

Um, thanks for letting me know, I guess . . .

NP!!

was so sweet for letting me know that   . Better to know now.

Are you kidding!? She's a HUGE !!! And just trying to keep you and apart.

No . . . Really? You think so???

ABSOLUTELY! She knows he ❤️ ❤️ you and doesn't want him marrying someone from a family like ours. is SO EMBARRASSING! But whatevs, will be back with 💍, no doubt.

I don't know . . .

Well, I'm out super early in the morning! Heading back to my humble little and the amazing . Thanks for having me!

Anytime.

Great! I'll be back in like 2 weeks.

Goody.

Guess what!?!?! I'm going to marry !

Seriously???

 Girl, I am 27!!!! At my age, he's a catch.

But what about ???

 I'll have and a husband with . I have about as much chance of happiness in marriage as most people do.

Did you hear the good news!?!?
 !!!

WHAT!? Impossible. He wants .

He's over that! He's marrying my now. Wahoo!!!

W.E. Just don't eye up my stuff when you're here!!! 😠👀

"Next to being married, a girl likes to be crossed a little in love now and then. It is something to think of, and it gives her a sort of distinction among her companions."

As it stands, Mrs. Bennet has had no luck marrying off her daughters to men of means. She was sure the rich and handsome Mr. Bingley would propose to her oldest and most beautiful daughter, Jane, but he has gone off to London with no set promise of return. Her second born, Elizabeth, has turned down Mr. Collins, a distant cousin who is to inherit the Bennet's Longbourn estate. And if that wasn't quite enough, Charlotte, the plain daughter of her "friend" Lady Lucas, was now to marry him. The only prospects that remain in town are the militia men whom the youngest Bennet girls have been chasing all summer. These are desperate times indeed.

Hey! Looks like we're staying in for the winter. ❄️ ❄️ ❄️

Oh, OK. Miss you.

 Oh totally! Miss you too. We've just been having so much fun with . She is the coolest! We just have SO much in common, and she and get along SO well.

👍

R U OK?

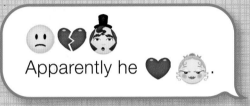 Apparently he

 That's ! Those sisters of his had something to do with this. Or worse,

Whatever. I'll get over it. Some day.

Thanks for hanging around these past few weeks and cheering up the fam!

I'm at your service! :)

 I'm also thankful everyone knows now what an absolute is. I'm glad your story came out!

It's a relief to have it out there! :D

 Well, every1 already hated him and liked you. They're relieved to hear they were right! :)

Hey! We're coming for our usual trip to . Can't wait to see u all tmrw!

Just in time! Everyone around here feels like about the whole  thing.

Poor girl. Maybe she can come back to with us after .

Oh, what a great idea!

I see the way you look at that . . . .

WHAT!?! OK, well maybe a little.

 You be careful of that one! He's handsome, funny, and broke. That's the worst combination.

I know, I know. I'll try not to encourage him.

I saw and she was juch a jerk.

She's always been a 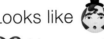! Ugh. I'm sorry.

 Looks like 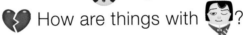 is gone forever. Sigh . . . How are things with ?

Don't be so sure about 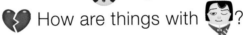!!! found a 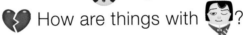 girl to flirt with, so that's over, too. I'm not really that , so I guess it wasn't really. Anyway, I'm visiting at, but I'm going to come through to see you first!

 Cool. 👍

- Wed, Mar 4, 1:28 PM -

 Thanks for having me in 🏰 ! But jeez, 👧 is really bummed, huh? ☹️

Yeah, we try to keep her busy, but you know . . . 💔 Speaking of keeping busy, want to go with us this summer to see the lakes? 🐎🚌 ☀️ 👍

 Sure! That sounds great! Thx!

Great!

- Sat, Mar 7, 11:42 AM -

 OMG! Your place is SO CUTE!!!

Thanks! I require a lot of alone time to make it just right.

 HA! Perfect.

Sooo, invited us for dinner tonight up at with her mom, .

Sounds like . . . fun?

- Sat, Mar 7, 7:18 PM -

 Dear Elizabeth, Do you play the piano? Please reply at once. This contraption is diabolical, and I demand to know my correspondences are going through! Sincerely, Lady Catherine

I do play .

Dear Elizabeth, How did you make that little picture? Do you write? Do you paint? You should do it all, you know! Regards, Lady Catherine

No, I don't do those things.

Dear Elizabeth, Didn't your governess teach you? With concern, Lady Catherine

We didn't have one of those . . .

Poorest Elizabeth, I have never heard of anything so absurd! So what do you girls do? Are your sisters out and about? Dolefully, Lady Catherine

Yup, we all are on the market.

To Elizabeth, Well, now I have heard it all. All five of you are out in society, looking for husbands at once. It's the height of impropriety! With alarm, Lady Catherine

Well, I don't see why the younger sisters should stay home just because the older ones haven't married yet. 😐

Attention Elizabeth: You've got some nerve to talk to me that way. How old are you anyway?
Cautiously, Lady Catherine

None of your beeswax! JK! 21.

To Elizabeth, JK?
Confusedly, Lady Catherine

Just kidding.

Guess who's coming to visit?

Who?

 ! He's coming to for Easter.

Greeeeaaaat.

How are you? How is the family doing?

You should know how is. She's been in for the past THREE MONTHS!! Haven't you seen her???

Oh, um, well, anyway. I'll see you around , I guess . . . and I will be here for a while.

See ya!

I'm glad to have someone else to talk to around here! 😜

Me too! 🙂

Things can be a bit of a 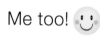 around these parts. 😲 💇‍♀️ 😴

You said it, not me! 😄 OK, going to try my hand at this 🎹. Let's see what words of wisdom 🐵 offers! 😜 😀

Stare down at me all you want, I'm not going to let you intimidate me out of playing well! 🎹 🎶 😐

HA! You don't really think I'm doing that, do you? That's a little 🍌🍌🍌.

LOL! I guess you're right. You just have a reputation of being bad around 🎶.

Ugh. Don't remind me. I'm sorry about that first night we met at the ball and I wouldn't 💃. I'm just shy! 😄

Uh-huh. Well, when I suck at , it's cuz I'm not practicing . . .

- Tue, Apr 7, 2:26 PM -

 I know someone who likes you!!!

Please. Who?

  of course!!!

Um, I don't think so.

 Well he was in no rush to leave when it was just the 2 of you talking at today, but then I show up, and bam, off like !!

LOL! That's cray cray!

 We'll see . . .

We're heading out this Saturday. If wants to anyway. I'm at his disposal. 😜

Well, he does look out for his friends. in particular.

 Oh yeah. That guy. I heard saved him from a bad 👰 recently. 😳

Is that so?

 Yeah, apparently there were some "strong objections" to her.

Gotta go.

- Thu, Apr 9, 5:03 PM -

 Didn't see you at at . You OK?

I have a headache.

 Oh no! I hope you feel better soon. So. Um. I love you. Marry me?

I've tried super hard not to feel this way. What with your family and social position and everything not exactly making the top notch, but I can't help it! I 🖤🖤🖤 you! So let's do this! 🏰🎆🖤

Um. NO!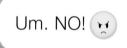

What? That's all you have to say? You're not even going to give me an actual reason?⁉️⁉️⁉️😕

Fine. 1. Your "proposal" was basically you calling me trash whom you happen to like. CLASSY!

2. You broke up and . I KNOW YOU DID THAT 💩!!!

3. You're the kind of guy who would deny your father's DEATHBED WISHES for !

 So that's what you think of me? I was just being HONEST when I proposed. Can you blame me for that? You're just upset it hurt your pride. 😡

There is literally no way under the ☀ or on 🌑 that you could have proposed that would have made me say yes.

FINE! Have a good life.

- Fri, Apr 10, 10:17 AM -

From: Darcy

To: Elizabeth

Subject: For the Record

Dear Elizabeth,

Don't worry, I'm not going to propose again or anything stupid like that.

I just want to set the record straight. I broke up 👰 and 👱 because after watching her closely, I didn't think she really 🖤 him, but he SUPER 🖤 her. And with 💰👒 and basically everyone predicting 💍, I thought it better to spare my friend from marrying someone pushed into the wedding by her fam, who was just after his 💰💰💰. You excluded, of course! You know her better than I do though, and if you say she really 🖤 him, then I'm sorry I didn't pick up on it. I never wanted to hurt her. She's 😎! And I'm sorry I didn't tell Bing that she was in 🏛️, but I'm NOT sorry that I tried to save my friend from a bad marriage.

Now, about 🧑. I'll tell you the truth. But this is for your 👀 only!! His dad, who was a great man, worked for my father. When my dad died, he left Wick a bit of 💷♠️ and told me to make sure Wick got a good gig in the ⛪. But Wick wanted to go into law, and said, "Gimme me the 💷♠️, and I'll never ask for help with the ⛪." Fine. I paid him. Three years later, he comes back with no law degree and a bad rep, begging me to get him into the ⛪. I always knew that was a bad idea for him, so I said no. 👎 So what does he do? He tries to get my sister, 👶, who was only FIFTEEN, to elope with him! I stopped it just in time. You can ask 🙂 if you don't believe me.

So, that's the story. I was too 😡 yesterday to tell it then. But there it is.

God bless,
Darcy

Where are you!?!? and are leaving!! They're at to say goodbye.

Oh, I'm just out walking . . .

 Well, just left, but is still hanging out, waiting to say goodbye.

Oh, I'm still walking in the gardens . Got a lot to think about. Do you think I'm prideful? What about prejudiced?

 What are you talking about!?!?!

Never mind.

- Sat, Apr 11, 6:35 PM -

 Dear Elizabeth, You seem unnaturally upset. I bet it's because you're going back home soon. Just write your mother and tell her you're staying longer. Charlotte would be very happy to have you stay. Regards, Lady Catherine

That's sweet, but I have to get back.

Dear Elizabeth, Surely your parents don't really need you at home. Warmly, Lady Catherine

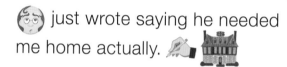 just wrote saying he needed me home actually.

Sweet Elizabeth, Fathers don't really need their daughters for anything. Stay another month, and I'll take you back to London myself. God bless, Lady Catherine

Thanks but no thanks. I really have to go. Honestly!!

To Elizabeth, At least have Mr. Collins send some servants with you or something. With concern, Lady Catherine

Thanks, but my uncle has it covered.

- Sat, Apr 18, 9:26 PM -

It was great having you stay with us!!!! I 🖤 🖤 🖤 SO MUCH!!! Don't you think we just make the best couple!?!?

I am really super happy for you both!! 😃 👏 😍

Thanks! It's like we share a brain!!! We just think the same things about EVERYTHING!!! Being married is AWESOME!!!! 👍❤️🎉

Uh-huh. Well, thanks for having me!

- Tue, May 5, 12:07 PM -

Hey! Glad we're going back to 🏰 together from 🏛️. Thanks for making the stop on your way from ⛪.

Me too! Will be great to get some hang time.

Yesssss! You'll have to tell me all about your summer.

Riiiiiight.

- Sun, May 10, 11:14 AM -

Yea!!!! I'm SO GLAD you and 👧 are coming home!!! 👻 and I will meet you at the inn. We ordered so much food and have done tons of shopping!!! 🍕🍕🍕🍰🛍️

It'll be good to see you, too! Wait, who are you bringing with you?

LOL! That's Kitty, duh. God, it's like she's invisible sometimes!

Oh. I forgot about her . . . How are things?

You mean other than my new awesome !? Well, the are leaving for the winter. Wickham and that girl split up. He's safe.....for now!!

I think you have that backward.

Huh? Well, whatever, I can't wait for you to see my new !

Sooooo . . . I have to tell you something. proposed. To me. In pretty much the least romantic way possible. Obviously I said no.

WOW. That is CRAZY! He must be so !!

I know. I feel bad, but I'm sure he'll get over it in no time. You know him!! OK, I also have to tell you something you can't tell ANYONE ELSE!!! OK???

OK, I just forwarded you part of an email wrote me about .

I don't believe anyone could be that rotten!! 🙊😷

I didn't believe it at first either, but it adds up!

Should we tell people??? They should know isn't that bad . . .

We can't!!! Think of . It would be SO embarrassing! 🙄

OMG! 's wife asked me to go to 🕌 with them! That's where all the 😈 are going. 😃 SHE IS SO COOL!!!!

Awesome!! You're going to have a SUCH a good time!! 😎

RIGHT!? But will not stop whining about not getting invited. LOL!

Who? Oh, ! She'll get over it! 😜

You're not seriously letting go to to follow the , are you???

Better she go there and act like a than do it here where she can embarrass us all.

 She's already embarrassed us all by being such a . . . you know!

What, did she scare away your boyfriend or something?

DAD! NO! Ew. She just flirts with anything with a pulse. She's also vain and kinda dumb. It's mortifying! And if we don't rein her in soon, she's going to find some real trouble. Mark my words. 😠

No one can think that badly of us as long as you and 👵 are around. And honestly, I'm looking forward to the peace and quiet! 😴

- Thu, May 28, 5:26 PM -

I'm heading out to 🕌 soon. I'll miss you! 😉 😘 How was ⛪ anyway?

I got to hang out with and .

 Really? You saw them a lot?

Oh, yes! They told me all sorts of interesting things!

 isn't so bad actually. Once you get to know him.

Well, you know how I feel about him. He was probably on his best behavior in front of . You know he's supposed to marry her daughter  right?

Yup! 😃

- Sat, Jun 6, 3:08 PM -

 is the 💣 !!! I love it here!!! ❤️❤️❤️❤️❤️

Good for you. 😐

I have been buying so many cute clothes!! 🛍 And the 🎩🎩🎩🎩!!! SO CUTE!!! Especially that 🧑!!! 🎩🖤

Isn't that just awesome for you.

Oh, gotta go! We're heading to the 🎩 🌃. EEEEEE!!!! 😍

- Tue, Jun 16, 11:22 AM -

So excited about our trip! Sorry to say we have to delay leaving a bit though. 🎩 has work. Ugh! 😢

That's cool! I'm just excited for the lakes. They're going to be so beautiful! 😃

Yeah, about that. We can't go for quite as long as we hoped, so we're just going to Derbyshire. Sorry!!! 😰 BUT we will get to see , which will be really cool! Too bad the owner, , will be away.

You sure that he won't be there???

That's the word around town.

"How humiliating is this discovery! Yet, how just a humiliation! Had I been in love, I could not have been more wretchedly blind! But vanity, not love, has been my folly."

Nothing besides Elizabeth's opinion of Darcy has improved much, but her opinion of herself—for having misjudged him so awesomely—has plummeted considerably. Jane's heart remains broken, Lydia continues to chase militia men, leaving Kitty at home with her jealousy, Mary continues her solitudinous studies, and Mr. and Mrs. Bennet's squabbling and bickering are injurious to the whole family. Now that Elizabeth's trip with her aunt and uncle has been shortened from a retreat to the Lake District to a short visit to Derbyshire, where Darcy's beautiful estate of Pemberley sits, all she has to look forward to are reminders of the life she could have had if she hadn't been so proud. Her only solace is that the master of the house will not be summering there.

I thought you said 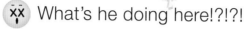 wasn't home!?!?! What's he doing here!?!?!

I guess he came home early. It is his house after all. You know him or something?

 A little . . .

Well, what's the problem? Everyone at  him.

 ●●●

No problem. Just surprised. 😶

- Tue, Aug 4, 3:32 PM -

It was great seeing you today! How have you been? How is your family? 😃

Hi. They're good. I'll introduce you to my uncle and aunt, . They're 🏛 merchants.

Awesome! I'd love to meet them! I'll see if your uncle wants to go fishing with me at my fav pond. Does he like fishing? It's a great spot!!

Great. I'm sure he'll like that a lot. 😃

Then you can meet . If you want to! She's super sweet and really wants to meet you.

Oh! Sure. That'd be great.

- Tue, Aug 4, 6:27 PM -

 So that 🙂 is a pretty cool guy! 😎

 Yeah, he was being really nice.

 From what 🙂 said, I thought he'd be a 😾. But he's 😇 . 😃

Yeah, 🙂 wasn't such a good guy after all. I've heard from reliable sources that he's pretty much 💩

 I could see that! We'll have a chance to get to know 🙂 and 😌 more now.

Hey, thanks for having us over on such short notice! I know you probably weren't expecting visitors first thing in the morning. ☀️ 🙂

NP! It was really great to meet you! 😃 👍 🎆

Well, thank you for being so cool. 🙏 I hope it wasn't too much to have 🎩 pop by like that, too. We were just full of surprises this morning!

LOL! It was great to see him. It'd been tooooo long.

Well, I hope you'll come to for  in a couple days . . . ?

Absolutely!

- Wed, Aug 5, 4:31 PM -

 SO GOOD TO SEE YOU TODAY!

You too! I can't believe how long it's been.

Right!? I'm super excited you're here. I have a lot of questions I want to ask you.

I can't imagine what about!

- Thu, Aug 6, 10:17 AM -

Hey, so I guess we're both in this week. How are you? 🤚

Fine. I was better yesterday, but whatever.

OK . . . well I guess I'll be seeing you around .

Can't wait. 😐

- Thu, Aug 6, 1:22 PM -

 Ugh, did you see what 😒 was wearing!?!?! 🙈 She's such a 🐷! And whatever happened to her boyfriend 👦??

I think she's nice. 🙂

Could have been any more boring!?!? And that dress. *SHALLOW*

 Dang it, autocorrect! I meant *SHUDDER*

Actually, shallow sounds more appropriate coming from you.

From: Jane

To: Elizabeth

Subject: WORST NEWS EVER!!!

Lizzy,

You're never going to believe this! Or maybe you will because you know this guy is a 💩. But 👳🏻‍♀️ and 😏 supposedly ran away to Scotland so they could get married without asking 👴🏻 👰🏼‍♀️ !!! As if that weren't bad enough, they never even showed up there!!! Now they're probably living in some fleabag hotel in 🏛️ . Wick's friend Denny said Wick probably never even meant to marry her. Just to, well, YOU KNOW!!!

😐 has looked EVERYWHERE and can't find them. He and his wife feel like total jerks, but it's not their fault. Ugh, this is THE WORST!!! No one will ever marry her after this, and no one will probably ever marry us either for that matter. 😵 😖 You have to come home, like NOW! 🐑 is in trouble for hiding that she knew Lyd 🖤 Wick, Mom won't leave her room, and I've never seen Dad so ☹️ in all my life!

Jane

Hey, how are you doing today?

OMG OMG OMG! I'm freaking out!!!!

 !?!?!?

 ran away with and you KNOW what that means.

Oh no! That's awful! Has anyone gone after her?

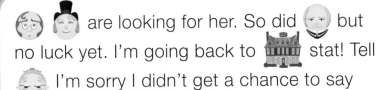 are looking for her. So did  but no luck yet. I'm going back to 🏛️ stat! Tell I'm sorry I didn't get a chance to say goodbye. 🙁

I wish I could help.

Thanks. I gotta go. 🐎🛒

Maybe this isn't so bad. 🧑 and 👒 are kind of suited for each other. He can't possibly mean to NOT marry her. That would be terrible! 💩 🙁

He'll never marry a girl with no 💰. He's a 🐍 and a 😣 !!!

But he'll get kicked out of the army for this! Maybe they can make him 💍 her . . . ?

Make a 😾 honorable? Unlikely!! But thanks. 😢

OUR LIVES ARE OVER!!!!!!!!!!!!

You have to calm down, Mom.

  is going to have to fight him, and he's going to DIE!!!!!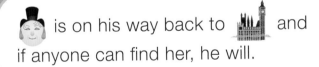

is on his way back to and if anyone can find her, he will.

I'm looking everywhere, but am having no luck finding  and .

  refuses to leave until he finds her.

You better keep him from doing anything stupid!!!!

I'm doing my best here! I've been talking to , who has already looked everywhere, to see if any of Wick's army buddies might know where he went.

KEEP TRYING!!!

Well, you should ask to ask  if he knows of any family  has in . That'd be our best shot!

!?!?!?

From: Mr. Collins

To: Mr. Bennet

Subject: HOW AWFUL!!!!

Hey Cuz,

I am so sorry to hear about little 👒!! What a terrible, awful, disastrous, lassivious (sp??), disgrace!!!! You must be SOOOOO EMBARRASSED!!! I know I would be! When I told them all about it, 🍄 and 👵 agreed with me that this is just about the worst thing that could happen. Imagine, had things gone differently, and, god forbid, I ended up marrying 👒, I'd be caught up in this whole 💩🌩 with you. Dodged that bullet! Am I right???
Want my advice, you should just disown the 🐩.

Lots of love!!!!

Mr. Collins

- Fri, Aug 14, 4:26 PM -

😔 is on his way home, but I'm still looking for 👒. 👀

You better be! At least didn't get .

  owes all over town from .

It just keeps getting better!

- Mon, Aug 17, 12:02 PM -

  has been found!!

Great!!! Dare I ask.....?

Afraid not. BUT they will get married if you agree to, well, pay them each year . . . Just a little!

WHAT!?!?! What about his debts?

They're paid. Don't ask.

OK . . .

- Mon, Aug 17, 12:14 PM -

 You have to get this resolved stat! Just agree to the stupid terms.

I know. It's just so nuts! must have paid 💰 to get 🧑 out of debt.

AND convince him to 💍 👩. There's no way he was going to marry a girl with no £ 👑 £.

I know! Ugh, I'm never going to be able to repay this debt. HATE. 😠

📷 made an arrangement for 📷 to 💍 📷 . He probably handed over a lot of 💰 💰 💰 and 📷 has to pay them annually.

EEEEEEEEE!! She is going to be a 👰 !!!!! I can't WAIT to buy her dress!!!!! I 🖤 that 📷 !!!!

Seriously? 📷 They both have been TERRIBLE, and Uncle and Father had to BUY this marriage. 😠

Well, your uncle's would have been ours if he had never been born, so it's only fair.

Wow.

I can't wait to tell EVERYONE!!!!

- Mon, Aug 17, 3:03 PM -

Thanks for working out our . . . situation.

Don't mention it!

 Well, I intend to pay you back every last .

Really, DO NOT mention that again. I'm serious. Just forget that part.

- Mon, Aug 17, 4:46 PM -

 I can't wait to see our little 👩 !!! 😃 💁 💜 I have SO much dress planning and shopping to do. She's coming home!!! 🏰 ❤️

I am not paying one penny for her dress!

 EXCUSE ME!!?!?!?

And she is NOT coming into this house!!!

 But she's our DAUGHTER! And she's going to be sent up North soon for 's promotion!!!

NO. End of discussion!

You have to let come here. I know it sucks, but it's the right thing to do. 😕

Give me one reason why it's the right thing to do. She's a DISGRACE!!!!

I know. But it's . What else can you expect? Just see her once before she moves into what will be a pretty miserable life. Then you can go on hating it as hard as you want to. 🙏

Sigh. Fine. But I won't enjoy it. 😢

OMG!!!!! Can you believe I'm MARRIED!?!?! Admit it! You = jealous!!! 😛

Don't you feel . . . ? Oh, never mind.

I just 🖤 🖤 🖤 my Wickypoo!!! The wedding was SO COOL!!! was even there!!!

WHAT!?!?!

Oops! I said too much. 🙈 😉

- Fri, Sep 4, 11:52 AM -

Hey! So this whole sitch is crazy! Glad it's all cleared up now though.

Seriously! All's well that ends well, I guess. 😐

So, uh, what was doing at the wedding? Seems strange he showed up, given the whole history and not being part of our side of the fam. 🙁

You don't know? I mean no one is supposed to know, but I thought YOU knew.

 I am totally clueless! What are you talking about!? 😐

WELL! 😭 left 🏛️ right after you. HE is the one who found the 🖤 🐦 🐦 . HE is the one who paid off the debts and bribed 😏 . Only after 👒 refused to leave 😉, that is.

 OMG!

Hey, uh, sis, how goes it? Did you have a nice time at ??

Yes, it was very enlightening.

Did you go to Kympton? You know, I was going to work for the there......

Yeah, I heard you screwed that up. Listen, let's just forget ALL that history and be cool moving forward. OK?

is coming back!!!!!

Great.

 You HAVE to go and visit him!!!!!

You said that last year and promised he'd marry one of the girls if I did. You made a fool of me then, and I won't do it again.

 OH, FOR THE......It's just POLITE!!

I give zero   about polite.

- Sat, Sep 19, 11:03 AM -

 Two guys are here. and that tall guy that's always around him. The one that was kind of a . . . ?

 is here???? Also, who is this???

 It's your DAUGHTER KITTY!!! Ugh. Why do I have no role in this story??? Anyway, yes, it's . They just got to town and they stopped by, I guess.

Oh, it's you . Hi. Ugh, that guy is the WORST! But, if he's Bing's friend, let's all just be cool. OK? 😎 🙏

- Sat, Sep 19, 3:52 PM -

Well, that was AWKWARD. 😳 Poor .

I KNOW!!! Can you believe how went on about ????

Like we should be PROUD of that! Ugh. SO EMBARRASSING!!! 🙈

Ugh!!! I just can't believe they agreed to come over for .

Seriously!! barely said anything! Why did he even come???

- Tue, Sep 22, 9:56 PM -

Well, you sure seemed to have a nice time with at dinner tonight!!!

Oh, don't be silly! We were just hanging out. NBD.

Uh-huh.

SERIOUSLY!! We are just friends. .

Suuuuuuuuure you are.

I'm not so dumb as to just fall for him again. I know nothing is there.

You're not the one who I saw falling!!!!

REALLY!!?!?

Guess what!?!?!

I have a pretty good idea, but you tell me!

 and I are engaged!!!!!!

HOORAY!!!!
I am SO SO happy for you!!!

I just wish you could find someone to make you this happy.

Oh, don't worry about me. Someday I'll find another . 🔫 ☠️ 😉

- Sat, Oct 3, 10:17 AM -

Dear Elizabeth, You keep your grubby middle-class hands off my nephew! I know your sister is marrying up, and everyone is saying you're going to gold-dig my nephew, but that is not going to happen. In earnest, Lady Catherine

Excuse me?

To Elizabeth, Do not play cute with me! I know your family is telling everyone who will listen that you're going to be his wife. Solemnly, Lady Catherine

Well, this is NEWS to me! But I have to say, you texting me with it makes me think it could actually happen!

Attention Elizabeth: Don't you point those fingers at me! Darcy is going to marry my daughter, so you just keep away from him! Significantly, Lady Catherine

Are they engaged?

Elizabeth: Well, yes and no. Not exactly, but his mother and I decided they'd get married, and so they will.
Determinedly, Lady Catherine

Well, your 's not to him, and neither am I.

ELIZABETH: Promise me it will stay that way. PROMISE!
With resolution and alarm, Lady Catherine

No way! If they're going to get together, then they'll get together. I have NOTHING to do with it.

ELIZABETH: Your family are a bunch of nobodies, and your little sister is . . . well, YOU KNOW! I can't let my nephew get involved with such YOU KNOW!
With undying hatred, Lady Catherine

OK, enough. GOODBYE!!!!

You have now blocked

I got the funniest email from ! He wrote to congratulate , whatever, blah blah blah, but then he wanted to warn me that will be pissed about YOUR engagement to, guess who!!?!!?

Um, who?

!!!! LOL!!!!! You guys are so obviously NOT into each other. I don't know why my cousin is so . Seriously, what a nut!

Hahahaha, yeah. Crazy . . .

Hey. I know this is sort of selfish of me, but it's killing me not to say anything.

I have to thank you for the whole thing. I know I'm not even supposed to know about it, but Lydia let it slip that you were at the wedding, and I made tell me the story. I just have to thank you on behalf of all us Bennets!!!!

I can't believe your aunt told you! I did it to make you . And because I was responsible for not letting 🌍 know what a 💩 that guy is. I feel exactly how I did last April, when, you know, 💍. Do you still feel the same?

I feel exactly opposite of how I did then!!! 🖤 🖤 And I'm SO embarrassed about what I said then. 🙄 😟

I am the one who's embarrassed. 😟 You told me I was being a jerk, and I was! I just assumed, that you'd say yes. I was raised to always expect yes.

So you didn't absolutely HATE me!?

I could never hate you! You showed me that I had to grow up. I never thought you'd like me though after I was such a . It was only after told me what you said that I decided I might have a shot with you.

And . I'm guessing you gave your on that?

After we came for dinner, I was sure she him after all, so I told him that I was a 💩 and wrong. He was SO relieved to hear he wasn't crazy and that she him. So then, well, 💍!

Speaking of 💍, will you marry me?

 YEEEEEESSSSSSSSSSSSSSSSSSSSSSS!!!!!!! 🖤🖤🖤🖤🖤🖤🖤🖤🖤🖤🖤

- Tue, Oct 6, 5:01 PM -

 Where were you today??? I haven't seen you in hours . . . 🕐

You're probably not going to believe me . . . but + me = 💍!!!!

 Come again??? I thought you hated that 💩 . . . ?

Nope! Totally 💜 him like freakin' crazy!!!

 I'm SO CONFUSED!!!! So you're happy? Should I congratulate you? 😕

I am BEYOND happy!

- Wed, Oct 7, 6:56 PM -

 Are you pulling my leg with this thing? I thought you hated him??

I was such a . I actually super him!!!

 I'm being very serious right now. Don't marry someone you don't like. Have you seen me and ? DO NOT end up like us.

Yikes. I know. And I super swear. I really do like him and him.

Alright, you've got my blessing ! Who am I to say no to a guy like him!?

Wed, Oct 7, 9:42 PM

OK, I have to tell you something. I'm engaged. To  . . .

Hello???

OMG!!!!! YOU'RE GOING TO BE SOOOOOO RICH!!!!!!! 🎰 💰 💰 💰 💰 💰 He is SO RICH! And TALL! And HANDSOME!!!!! CONGRATULATIONS!!!!!! 💰 🎉 💜! 💰 🎉 💜! 💰 🎉 💜! I'm going to lose my 💩 I'm so HAPPY!!!!!!!!

 Thanks, Mom.

- Wed, Oct 9, 2:11 PM -

 So, why did you ever start to me in the first place??

You're !!!!

I think it's because the other girls are all, "Oh, I 🖤 you, you're so 😎!!!" And I was like "you're a 💩". 😛

Speaking of 💩, when are you going to tell ??

I'll e-mail her now. It's not going to be pretty, but she'll get over it. 🔫💀🔪

"Happy for all her maternal feelings was the day on which Mrs. Bennet got rid of her two most deserving daughters."

In the ultimate happily ever after, Jane and Elizabeth married Misters Bingley and Darcy respectively on the same day. They were then mistresses of lavish estates, and their parents, particularly their mother, could not have ended up happier. Their youngest sister, Kitty, became quite the lady herself thanks to the company of her two sisters and their superlative society. She was able to unlearn all the bad behavior she had gleaned from Lydia, who unsurprisingly wrote from the North with congratulations to Elizabeth and her hand out. Mary, being left home alone often with Mrs. Bennet, even managed to creep out of her shell just a little bit. So it was that all the relations and relationships that emanated from the Bennets exemplified the rare and prized features of love and happiness.

I've given this a lot of thought. It IS proper for Dad to go and introduce himself to Mr. Bingley. It is the accepted social custom, and it could potentially alleviate any awkwardness. 🤝👍

It wouldn't, however, benefit any of the women here as such an introduction would likely result in frivolous activities, useless flirtations, and time better spent learning. ✍️

Hello? Mother?

GEORGIANA DARCY

The Hero's Shy Sister

LADY CATHERINE DE BOURGH

The Hero's Rich and Mean Aunt

NETHERFIELD PARK

LONGBOURN

PEMB

ANNE DE BOURGH

The Ever-Sick Daughter
of Lady Catherine

MR. COLLINS

The Worst

RLEY

HUNSFORD

LONDON